USBORNE
FAIRY
TALES
for BEDTIME

Retold by
Mary Sebag-Montefiore

Illustrated by
Elena Selivanova, Raffaella Ligi
and Brooke Boynton-Hughes

CONTENTS

CINDERELLA

Cinderella

Long, long ago, in a faraway kingdom, a girl lived with her father, stepmother and two stepsisters. She was named Cinderella, because her stepmother made her work in the kitchen where the fire spattered her with ashes and cinders.

"Cinderella!" her stepmother screeched all day long. "Sweep the floor! Scrub the dishes! Peel the vegetables... NOW!"

Her stepsisters whined, "Cinderella! Mend my dress! Clean my shoes! Wash my underwear! Slowcoach, lazybones, do it NOW!"

They ordered her about as they lay on sofas in their frilly frocks.

Cinderella's only dress was ragged and patched. She slept in the attic on a bed of straw, while her stepsisters had soft velvet divans and silk sheets. Their bedrooms were painted in the latest style, with crystal chandeliers, and gold mirrors on every wall.

These mirrors were so vast, they could see themselves from head to foot. And what did the mirrors show?

Alas! Two ugly girls. Two pairs of spiteful eyes. Two scornful mouths.

But when Cinderella dusted the glass, it reflected a girl with a sweet and loving expression, a thousand times more beautiful than her stepsisters, despite her shabby clothes.

"I wish my father would help me," she used to think, but he was meek, weak, and completely under his wife's thumb.

He didn't know his new
wife and her daughters had a
cruel streak until he'd
married, and then
it was too late.
One day, the
younger stepsister
marched into the
kitchen, wrinkling up her
large nose in disgust.

"Ugh. It's horrible here. All dark and dirty. Cinders, we want you to do our hair. NOW!"

"Yes, of course," said Cinderella, putting down her broom to follow her. "But why?"

"It's none of your business, but I'll tell you, because you must make us look wonderful. We've been invited to THE ball!

It's the ball of the season, the Prince's ball at the Palace. The King and Queen say it's time he was married. Just think, his bride might be ME!"

By this time, they were in her bedroom. The elder sister pushed the younger one aside.

"Not you, ME! Do MY hair first, Cinders, because I'm older."

"But I went down into that smelly kitchen to find her."

When they had finished squabbling, they screamed at Cinderella: "Bring us combs, curling tongs, ribbons, flowers and feathers, NOW! We have to look unique."

Cinderella spent the next few days inventing hairstyles. She designed ballgowns, bought material and stitched away, as well as doing her usual tasks of scrubbing, cooking and cleaning, while her stepmother constantly nagged, "Hurry up, Cinderella! Oh, what did I do to deserve such a lazy girl?"

Cinderella

On the day of the ball,
Cinderella helped her
stepsisters to dress.
They insisted on being laced
tightly into their gowns, so
they'd appear slimmer; tottering
on high heels so they'd seem
taller. They rouged their cheeks,

blackened their eyebrows, and painted their lips scarlet.

"Aren't my darlings simply gorgeous?" cooed their mother.

The sisters were extremely pleased with themselves. "Don't you wish you were coming, Cinders?" they asked as they left.

"What a joke!" their mother said. "You're grand young ladies.

She's nothing
but a servant."
And with loud
guffaws, the
three of them
swept away.
"Yes," thought Cinderella,
clearing up the mess they'd left,
"I wish I *could* go to the ball."
Then, exhausted, she sat by
the kitchen fire, gazing at the

glowing flames, imagining she
was part of the fun. She could
almost hear the music, almost
smell the garlands of flowers,
almost see the Prince... and
then reality – her
dirty clothes, the
dingy kitchen,
her loneliness
– seemed to mock
her pretendings.

It was more than she could bear
and she began to cry.

And then...

THEN...

"Magic?" whispered Cinderella,
her eyes huge with astonishment.

For out of the smoke of the
fire, a woman stepped forward,
dressed in pale fluttery robes,
with wings to match.

"Never lose
hope, my
child," said
this apparition,
waving the wand
she held in her hand. "You
SHALL go to the ball."

"Who... who are you?"
stuttered Cinderella.

"I am your fairy godmother,"

she said with a friendly smile. "Now, find me a pumpkin in the garden."

Cinderella was so amazed that she obeyed, though she couldn't see how a pumpkin could help.

The fairy tapped it with her wand, and it turned into a shining golden coach.

"I see six mice in your mousetrap," the fairy observed.

Cinderella

"Please set them free."

Each mouse, as it darted out, received a tap from the wand, and was instantly transformed into a dappled horse.

"We need a coachman..." mused the fairy.

"There's a rat in the trap," said Cinderella eagerly.

"Splendid! Bring it here!"

Cinderella
returned with a
large rat which
became a plump,
jolly coachman.
Six lizards were changed into six
elegant footmen with powdered
wigs, who jumped up to the
coach as though they'd done
so all their lives.

"Now," said the fairy, "you can travel to the ball."

"But my clothes..." pleaded Cinderella, holding out her dirty, ragged dress.

"Ah!" smiled the fairy, touching her with her wand.

Cinderella's rags vanished. In their place was a silver balldress, and shining on her feet were the prettiest, most

sparkling shoes in the world,
made entirely of glass.

"Thank you, Godmother!"
she sighed, twirling
around with joy.
"You've made
my dreams
come true."

"You look
lovely," replied
the fairy.

"Enjoy yourself, but return by midnight, or your coach will be a pumpkin again, your horses mice, your coachman a rat, your footmen lizards, and you will be dressed in your rags."

As Cinderella entered the ballroom, there was a profound silence. Momentarily, the dancing ceased and the music stopped. All were spellbound by her beauty. No one knew who she was, and she kept her identity secret.

The Prince asked her to dance, again and again, and as the hours passed, she knew herself to be in love. She could hardly believe she was whirling in the Prince's arms around the candlelit palace ballroom, instead of slaving in the kitchen at home.

"I shall hold another ball tomorrow night. Please come."

He smiled and kissed her hand.

"Maybe," said Cinderella, catching sight of her stepsisters. She waved, but they didn't recognize her.

"Tell me who you are," begged the Prince, but just then the clock struck eleven and three quarters, and Cinderella ran down to her golden coach.

The next day, the
stepsisters boasted
about the ball. "It was
a great success. A beautiful
princess waved to us. Now help
us prepare for tonight, Cinders."

"Certainly," said Cinderella.
"I wish I could go too."

"YOU? A dirty drudge?"
they sneered.

That evening, Cinderella waited by the fire, hoping... dreaming... longing...

Sure enough, her fairy godmother appeared as before, and this time she dressed Cinderella even more magnificently in a ballgown made of gold and sewn with hundreds of diamonds.

Cinderella

Cinderella had diamond stars
in her hair – and on her feet,
the precious glass slippers.

"Don't forget," warned the
fairy. "Return by midnight."

"I promise," said Cinderella,
but she was too happy to
remember to look at the clock.

Twelve times it chimed,
marking the midnight hour.

"I must go!"
cried Cinderella,
her dress starting
to change as she
fled. In her haste,
she lost a shoe.

The Prince raced
outside, but there was
not a sign of her, nor her golden
coach and prancing horses.

"Where is she?" he asked. "Someone must have seen her." But everyone he asked shook their heads.

"We only saw a servant girl in rags running through the streets."

Retracing his steps, his head bent in sorrow, the Prince spied, glistening on the stairs, her glass slipper. He picked it up gently.

Now, at least, he had a clue. "The lady whose foot fits this shoe shall be my bride," he declared. "And I will not rest till I find her."

Cinderella ran all the way home, with nothing left of her finery but the other glass slipper, and arrived just before her stepmother and stepsisters.

They were gossiping about
the beautiful stranger, who
fled as the clock struck twelve,
and the Prince's sadness.
Cinderella's heart ached with
love and longing; her eyes
burned hot with unshed tears.

The next day, trumpeters
marched through the streets,
calling for every girl in every

house in the kingdom to try on
the glass slipper.

The stepsisters were overjoyed.
"Now's our chance," they cried.

"Oh dear," said their mother.
"Your feet are huge, with bunions,
and I hear the shoe is tiny…"

"We'll see about that," snapped
the sisters, splashing their feet in
icy water to shrink them.

They cut their toenails so
short they bled, and then curled
their toes over tightly.

At last, the Prince arrived at
their house with the shoe.

The stepsisters fought
each other to be the
first to try it, and
did all they could
to make it fit, but it
simply wouldn't go on.

Then Cinderella stepped
forward. "May I try?"

"You?" laughed her
stepmother. "A grubby servant?
Certainly not."

"Every girl must try," said
the Prince. Cinderella's foot
slipped into the
shoe as easily
as if it had
been made

for her, which of course it had.
Then she took the other shoe
from her pocket.

At that moment, her fairy
godmother appeared, touching
Cinderella with her wand,
which transformed her rags into
a dress. It was more wonderful
than any of the dresses before, as
white and pure as a bridal gown.

Cinderella

Her stepsisters and stepmother now recognized Cinderella as the beautiful stranger from the ball. They flung themselves on their knees, crying, "Forgive us! We should never have been so mean."

"Of course I forgive you," Cinderella smiled and the Prince then knew he had found a bride as good as she was beautiful.

After the wedding, Cinderella found her stepsisters a place at court, whereupon they each married a lord, and became much nicer.

As for Cinderella and her Prince, theirs was the marriage of dreams, filled with love and told in stories ever after.

JACK AND THE BEANSTALK

Jack and the Beanstalk

Once, there was a mother and her son, Jack. They lived in a sad tumbledown cottage and were desperately poor. Every day, their life grew worse.

The mother sold everything she had to get money – her hens and geese and most of the furniture.

She even sold the knives and forks. Only their cow Milky White was left, though she was old and gave hardly any milk.

Jack's mother wept at the empty rooms but Jack skipped around, laughing, "This is fun."

"There's more to life than fun, you silly boy," snapped his mother. "You're HOPELESS."

"I'm not," said Jack.

His mother sighed. "You'll have to take Milky White to market tomorrow, Jack. We can't afford to feed her. And mind you get a good price."

So the next day, Jack led Milky White along the road, dreaming of the wonderful things he'd buy with the money he'd make.

On the way, he met a strange-looking man with a wild, long beard and penetrating eyes.

"What a fine animal," said the man. "Here's a bargain for you, boy: you give me the cow, and I'll give you these." And putting his hand in his pocket, he drew out five large, shining beans.

"Not enough!" began Jack.

Jack and the Beanstalk

The man wagged a bony finger. "She's not a young cow, is she? Not much milk there. No one will buy her. You'd better take my beans. They're special."

Jack thought about it. Yes, Milky White was past her best. And the beans had seemed to glow. So he exchanged the cow for the beans and went home.

"How much did you get?" his mother asked, pouncing on him as he stepped through the door.

Jack opened his fist to show her, the beans now looking ordinary in his hand.

"How COULD you be so daft?" she shouted.

She snatched the beans and threw them out of the window.

"We're even worse off now, and it's ALL YOUR FAULT! You can't even sell a cow."

They both went supperless to bed, the mother silent with disappointment.

And Jack?

"I'm NOT hopeless," he thought angrily before he went to sleep. "Just wait and see…"

When he woke, his room was dark as night. "That's odd," he thought, "because I've slept long enough for it to be morning."

He peered out of the window. At least, he tried to...

The window was completely
blocked by enormous leaves.
Pushing them aside, he saw they
sprang from a mass of thick
stalks twisted together so that
they made a ladder. Upwards
stretched the ladder in a winding
green chain, up and up into the
sky until it was lost in the puffy
white clouds of infinity.

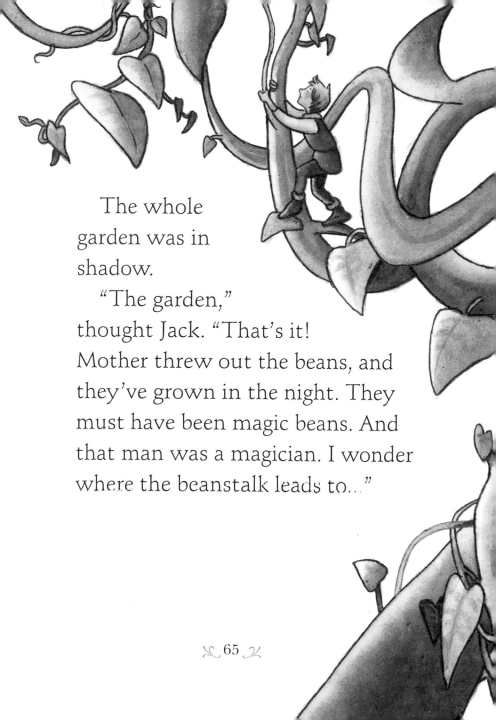

The whole
garden was in
shadow.

"The garden,"
thought Jack. "That's it!
Mother threw out the beans, and
they've grown in the night. They
must have been magic beans. And
that man was a magician. I wonder
where the beanstalk leads to..."

He dressed quickly and tested
out the beanstalk. Each step
enticed him on to the next. He
felt as fast and light and nimble
as a lizard running up a wall.

Higher and higher he climbed
among the rustling leaves, until
the air grew colder and clearer
and the sky more blue.

At last, he reached the clouds

and there the beanstalk came to
an end. He stepped off it onto
land, barren as a desert, not a
tree nor bush nor living thing
to be seen, no houses, no shops,
nothing familiar at all.

Jack was exhausted. But he
didn't want to go home without
exploring. "There must be
something here," he reasoned.

On he trudged. Eventually, he
spied a huge castle. He marched
to the door, climbed up to ring the
bell and scrambled back down.

The door opened slowly, and
an enormous woman poked her
head out, looking very surprised.

"Who are you?" she demanded.
"Don't you know this is a giant's
castle? My husband eats people!

Jack and the Beanstalk

He's out now, hunting for fresh human flesh. You'd make a nice little first course. WHY HAVE YOU COME?"

"I-I'm hungry," stammered Jack. "I'm sorry to disturb you, but could you spare something for me to eat? And don't let him eat *me*, Madam, I beg you."

She thought for a moment,

then beckoned him in. "I'll hide you in the bread oven. You're a polite boy. Brave, too. Yes, you're worth saving."

She led him through a vast hall to a massive kitchen that smelled of newly-baked bread, opened the oven and shoved Jack in with a plate of warm crusts. Then she clanged the grill door shut.

Just in time.
In thumped
the giant, huffing
like a gale force
wind, his footsteps thudding
like thunderclaps.

"Wife, bring me food," he
boomed, slumping onto an
enormous chair.

The woman sprang forward

with plates tottering with hunks of meat, whole cabbages, entire cakes and bowls of pudding.

Slurp, chomp, chew, swallow, went the giant until he was satisfied, and let out a stinky burp so evil-smelling that Jack, quivering in the oven, felt sick.

Then, sniffing the air, the giant started to bellow.

Jack and the Beanstalk

"FEE FI FO FUM
I SMELL THE BLOOD OF
AN ENGLISHMAN."

"I don't think you do, dear,"
said his wife. "No one's been
here all day."

"Oh, all right," said the giant.
"Bring me my hen."

Jack stared as the wife brought
out an ordinary brown hen.

She set it on the table before him. Every time the giant said, "Lay!" the hen squatted and produced a golden egg. The giant played with the hen all evening, until he had a pile of golden eggs.

"That's enough," he yawned at last, revealing huge, yellow teeth, and he stomped out of the kitchen with his wife.

Jack held himself still until he was sure they weren't coming back. Then he hopped out of the oven, seized the hen, and ran out of the kitchen, through the vast hall, out of the door, across the barren wastes, and down the beanstalk into his own garden.

He raced inside to tell his mother where he'd been.

"Look at this! Lay! Lay! Lay!" he commanded, and a stream of eggs dropped from the hen in a golden cascade.

"Oh, Jack, you clever boy!" she exclaimed, clapping her hands with joy. "Now we can mend the roof, buy food...

We'll be comfortable!"
 And so they
were. But after
only a few weeks,
Jack started to
grow restless.

 "I'm going up
the beanstalk
again, Mother. I
won't be long."

"Must you? Will you be safe?
That giant will want revenge."

"I'll outwit him," Jack said,
with a laugh. "I'll dye my hair
and change my clothes. I'll be
fine, you'll see."

So Jack climbed the beanstalk to the castle and knocked sharply on the door. Again, the giant's wife answered.

"Could you spare me a crust of bread?" whined Jack, in a completely different accent.

"I'm not sure," she said. "A boy came here not so long ago, who turned out to be a little thief."

"I'm not like that," coaxed Jack. "Oh, please...?"

At last, she consented, and this time she hid him in the kitchen dresser cupboard. Jack crouched there all evening, watching through a hole in the

wood as the giant stomped in,
and gulped down his supper.
Then, just as before, he sniffed
the air and trumpeted,
   "Fee Fi Fo Fum
   I smell the blood
   of an Englishman.
   Be he alive or be he dead,
   I'll grind his bones
   to make my bread."

"You're always right, dear,"
said his wife. "Just not good with
smells. There's no one here."

"Oh, all right," said the giant.
"Bring me my money bags."

The wife brought him
two bags, and left the room.
Chuckling, the giant tipped the
contents onto the table in a
jingling, glittering heap.

Jack and the Beanstalk

He counted the coins for ages,
then tied them up again in the
bags, and dozed off, snoring.
Rattle, spittle, whoosh, sounded
the snores.

When Jack was certain that the
giant's sleep was as profound as
the deep blue sea, and the snores
as regular as waves crashing to
shore, he crept from the cupboard,

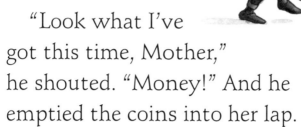

grabbed both bags,
and raced home.

"Look what I've
got this time, Mother,"
he shouted. "Money!" And he
emptied the coins into her lap.

"We're rich!" she whispered,
clinking them through her
fingers in a shining waterfall.
"You're a wonderful son!"

They lived happily for a few
months, until Jack began to long
to go up the beanstalk again.

"Don't, Jack," begged his
mother. "It's dangerous.
And we have more
than enough."

"But I want to,"
said Jack, kissing
her goodbye and
beginning his climb...

As before, he persuaded the
giant's wife to take him in. This
time she hid him in the sink.

Jack watched the giant
guzzle a mound of pies and
gulp so much ale that he
swayed where he sat. Then he
roared in a thick voice,
"WIFE, I REALLY
DO SMELL
FRESH MEAT!"

He stumbled around the kitchen, feeling in every crevice till he reached the sink. Luckily, he couldn't concentrate properly, and every time he touched Jack, Jack slid away from his jabbing, questing fingers in slimy rivers of soap bubbles.

"I'm sure I felt something," muttered the giant.

Jack and the Beanstalk

"Never mind, dear," soothed his wife, drying his hands, placing a golden harp in them and leading him to his chair.

The giant sank down with a sigh. "Play," he ordered, and the harp began to play, all by itself, such wonderful music that Jack yearned to listen to it for the rest of his life.

"Stop," murmured the giant, and as the music ceased, he was fast asleep and snoring. *Rattle, spittle, whoosh...*

Jack hauled himself out of the sink, seized the harp, and began to run.

But the harp's magic was not yet done. "Master," it called out. "MASTER! Help me!"

Instantly the giant awoke.

"MY PRECIOUS HARP," he yelled, lumbering after Jack. He roared with anger as he saw Jack disappear down the beanstalk.

"You're the one!" he yelled, shaking his fist. "It was YOU! You stole my hen and my money, and now my harp. I'll GET YOU!"

Grabbing hold of the swaying beanstalk, he started to climb.

Down the beanstalk whizzed Jack as fast as he could. Carefully, he set down the harp, then shouted, "Bring out one of the axes, Mother. Please hurry!"

THWACK!

Jack hacked fiercely at the beanstalk. It shook... It swayed...

It snapped! The giant tumbled to the ground, dead.

After that, Jack and his mother lived in peace and comfort. And everywhere Jack went, he was known as Jack the Bold, the boy who climbed the beanstalk, and made his mother smile.

THE ELVES AND THE SHOEMAKER

The Elves and the Shoemaker

There was once a shoemaker who lived with his wife in a busy town full of shops. For years, the business went well. He loved his work, and spent hours making beautiful shoes.

Then disaster struck. Another shoe shop opened up in the town, selling lots of cheaper shoes, and everyone went there. No one came to the shoemaker, and he and his wife grew poorer and poorer.

Winter came. The evenings grew dark. Then the snow fell, with icy winds. The shoemaker and his wife shivered in their freezing little house, once so snug and warm, because they couldn't afford to buy any more firewood.

One evening, the wife went to her husband, holding out an empty purse.

Her eyes drooped with worry.

"Oh my love, the worst has happened. We haven't any money at all. Not a penny left. What can we do?"

She flung open the doors to the empty kitchen cupboard. "Nothing there either," she wept.

"What shall we eat tomorrow?"

The shoemaker sat down with his head in his hands. "I wish I knew. I don't know where to turn. I'm so sorry."

"It's not your fault my dear," his wife said, with a sigh.

She began to slice an old, dry
loaf of bread, which was all
they had for supper.

"I've just enough leather left
to make one pair of shoes,"
said the shoemaker. "It's green.
I'll cut it out, and leave it on
my workbench ready for the
morning. Things are always
better in the morning."

The Elves and the Shoemaker

He tried to sound cheerful, because he didn't want his wife to know how unhappy he was. No one would really want green shoes, he was certain. But it was the only leather he had.

"Yes dear," said his wife, not wanting him to know, in her turn, that her worries were eating her up like a hungry ogre wolfing down his lunch.

"Things are never as bad as they seem," they comforted each other, but they both went to bed that night shivering, with fears unspoken and tears unshed.

They tossed and turned as the
wind howled through the cracks
in the roof, and snow slithered
into their bedroom through a
broken window pane, until at
last they fell asleep.

The next morning, they went silently downstairs, each secretly wondering what misery the day would bring. And there, on the bench, was a sight they never expected and one they would never forget.

"Look!" the shoemaker shouted. "Shoes! Just sitting there, exactly where I left the leather last night."

The shoemaker's wife picked one up in her hand, amazed. "What exquisite workmanship," she murmured.

The shoes were embroidered in fine gold and silver thread.

The Elves and the Shoemaker

They had jewels all over, even on the heels, and were edged in bronze.

"Who could have done it?" asked the shoemaker. "Only a master craftsman working better than his best. No one I know could have produced a shoe as fine as this. Who has been here, in the night, without us knowing or seeing or hearing?"

He stroked the shoes, and put them in the window. As soon as he did, a crowd of people collected outside, all pointing and exclaiming and gasping with wonder.

The shoemaker and
his wife could hear them.
"Beautiful!" "Unbelievable!"
"Unique!"
Then the richest lady
in the town pushed
her way through into
the shop. "I MUST
have these divine
shoes," she squealed.

"And I don't care how much they cost."

She emptied a purseful of gold into the shocked shoemaker's hands, seized the shoes, and sprinted down the street, calling over her shoulder, "I'll wear them at the ball tonight with my new green dress!"

The shoemaker and his wife laughed with relief. They'd made more money in one morning than they had in months.

They went out and bought a pile of firewood, and sausages and milk and tea and bread, and enough leather for two more pairs of shoes.

Red leather and shining black.

Again, the shoemaker cut out the leather, and left the pieces on his workbench to make up in the morning.

And when they came downstairs the next day, what did they see?

A pair of red high-heeled shoes, sewn with tiny stitches, studded with rubies, and finished with a silver buckle. And a pair of soft black slippers, fastened with velvet bows.

"Again?" whispered the shoemaker. "But WHY? And HOW? And WHO?"

"Don't ask," said his wife.

The Elves and the Shoemaker

"Just accept and be glad."

They put the shoes in the window as before, and once more, the shoes sold in minutes.

The shoemaker used the money to buy more leather of the very best quality, enough

for four new pairs.
He bought enough
brown leather to
make a pair of boots,
as well as white and purple and
yellow. He cut them all out and
laid them ready on the bench.

As they climbed the stairs that
night, his wife tried to stop them
both from hoping too much.

"It won't happen again," she said gently. "We mustn't expect the magic a third time."

When they came downstairs
the following morning, they
hardly dared look...

But there were four perfect
pairs laid out. Brown boots
edged with fur and shining like
chestnuts. Purple leather brogues
with purple laces. Yellow dancing
shoes. And the white leather now
shone in the morning sun.

Sparkling with diamonds and covered in lace, this pair was fit for a princess bride.

Once again, the shoes sold quickly for lots of money. After that, the magic happened every night. Whatever the shoemaker cut out in the evening, he found made up into shoes the very next morning.

Party shoes, baby shoes, old men's shoes, old lady's shoes, shoes for work, shoes for play, inexpensive shoes, everyday shoes and glittering shoes studded with jewels.

The townspeople flocked to the shop. More customers journeyed to buy the shoes from many miles away.

Everyone
was talking
about the
wonderful
shoes, and
the old
shoemaker
and his wife
grew happy
and rich.

One night, just before Christmas, the shoemaker said to his wife, "Why don't we stay up tonight, and see who it is who works for us?"

"I've been longing to know," she agreed. And so, after supper,

and after the
shoemaker
had cut out
his leather and
laid it on his
workbench, they
hid in a corner,
as quiet as they
could be behind
the curtain.

And they began to watch.

At midnight, they saw two little men, barefooted and dressed in rags, run in.

One carried a bag, which he put down before picking up a piece of leather that gleamed like glossy blackcurrants.

"Hmm," said the other. "What shall we make from that?"

The Elves and the Shoemaker

"Elves?"
thought the
shoemaker
in surprise.
"They're elves!"
thought his wife,
with delight.
Whispering and nodding,
the elves began to stitch and
embroider and pierce and

hammer so cleverly with
their quick little fingers
that the shoemaker and
his wife could scarcely
believe their eyes.

As they worked,
the elves delved
into their bag and
brought out jewels,
beads and ribbon,

fur trimming, silk lining, and
buckles and buttons of every
size and shade. Snip, snip, stitch
and hammer they went, all
night long, until several pairs of
perfectly finished shoes stood
on the workbench. Then they
jumped up and ran off.

The next day, the shoemaker's
wife turned to her husband.

The Elves and the Shoemaker

"We ought to do something to thank the little men. They've made us rich, and we should show how grateful we are. And it's nearly Christmas – a good time for a present. Why don't we make them each a suit of clothes? After all, they were wearing rags. They must be cold, running around in the winter night."

"That's an excellent idea, wife," said the shoemaker. "You make the clothes, and I'll make them each a pair of shoes."

All day, they were busy making the outfits.

Late that evening, they laid their gifts on the workbench and hid themselves once again, watching and waiting...

When midnight came, the little men ran in. They scrabbled around, searching.

They looked at each other, puzzled, for of course there were no leather pieces on the table.

And then, they spied the two neat piles of little clothes, and two pairs of tiny shoes. Instantly, they put them on and threw their old rags in the fire.

Then they danced around and around, jumping over the chairs, singing.

"What fine and
dandy
boys are we!
No longer workmen
shall we be."

Laughing, they ran out of the
door, singing all the way down
the street, till at last the echoes
of their song and their laughter
faded to silence in the still night.

The shoemaker and his wife
never saw the elves again. But
that didn't matter. They had
been lucky, and had shown
their appreciation.

Good fortune stayed with them from that moment on, and whatever they did forever afterwards, they did well.

PUSS IN BOOTS

One late summer's day, an old miller was riding back to his mill where he lived with his three sons. As he passed by a lake, he saw a tail splashing in the water, and turned his horse to take a closer look.

To his dismay, he saw a huge
water snake struggling with
its prey, a handsome cat. The
poor cat was spluttering and
meowing in sad little chokes.

The miller instantly jumped
into the water, uncoiled the cat,
and threw the snake back into
the lake, where it sank below
the surface, unharmed.

"Thank you,"
said the cat,
rubbing itself dry.

"You can talk?"
exclaimed the miller.

"I am magic," replied the cat.
"And in return for your kind
deed, I'll live with you and make
you rich. My power of speech,
however, must be our secret."

"Certainly," agreed the miller, making room for the cat on his saddle, and together they rode home to the mill.

"You must be good to our new cat," the miller told his sons when he got back. "Will you promise?"

"Of course," smirked the elder two, but did they mean it? No. They kicked him and teased him.

It was the youngest son
who gave the cat tasty
morsels and always
half of his own milk.

The years passed and the miller
died. He left his mill, his horse,
and his large fortune to the first
two sons; the third got the cat.

"Ha! Ha!" laughed the elder two
at their brother. "We're rich!

You and that silly old cat are nothing! We don't want either of you here."

The youngest son had loved his father, and his home. Now he had neither. Sad and lonely, carrying the cat and with only a few coins in his pocket, he left home forever.

"Don't worry," said a voice.

"Troubles are often a blessing in disguise. Buy me a pair of boots and a bag, and you'll see."

It was the cat who spoke.

The youngest son was amazed. "You c-can TALK!" he stuttered.

The cat nodded. "Now, my dear new master, obey my words and your dreams will come true."

With that, the cat leaped down and began walking on two legs, calling over his shoulder: "Come with me."

"Why not?" thought the young man.

He followed the cat until they
reached a dark cave.

"Here we'll stay, for the
moment," said the cat. "Now
bring me the boots and the bag."

The young man did as he was
asked, spending his last coins
on a large leather bag and a pair
of highly polished boots, and
bringing them back to the cave.

The cat
immediately
pulled the boots
on. "They're
wonderful," he purred,
gazing at his legs. "Almost
military. How impressive I look!
Everyone will respect me. Now
wait here until I return," he added,
slinging the bag over his shoulder.

Off he ran in his high top boots,
picking ripe corn from the fields
and putting it in the bag. When
he'd collected enough, he stopped
by a reedy part of the river where
swans nested. He opened the
bag, and lay beside
it, hidden by a
bush. Soon a pair
of beautiful swans

climbed inside, unable to resist such golden temptation.

Quickly, the cat trapped them alive, drawing tight the bag strings. He raced to the King's palace, bowed to the courtiers and displayed his catch.

"My master, the Marquis of Carabas," he announced, "sends me with these swans as a gift.

They are for His Majesty the King to ornament the palace lake."

"A talking cat! Extraordinary!" cried the courtiers. "His Majesty will be very interested." And they took the cat to the King.

"A fine gift," said the King. "But why," he asked the cat, "doesn't the Marquis of Carabas come to court, as the other courtiers do?"

Puss in Boots

"He says one comes across such an uncertain mixture of people," drawled the cat.

"He's absolutely right," agreed the King. "But why, I wonder, send a cat instead of a servant?"

"Ah!" replied the cat. "He finds normal servants too common. I am more unusual. My master is a man of fine taste."

"So I see," said the King, and he handed the cat a purse full of gold coins.

That night, the cat and his master enjoyed a delicious dinner of roast chicken, bought with some of the King's money.

"This is just the beginning," purred the cat.

The next day, the
cat went hunting
again. This time he
caught a peacock in
his bag, with glowing
emerald green feathers, each with
a sapphire blue eye. He took it
straight to the King, saying,
"This gift is from the Marquis
to enhance the royal garden."

"Very nice too," said the King graciously, giving the cat another fat purse of gold. "I'd like to meet your master."

The cat bowed and left. As he went out, he noticed the King's daughter. Never had he seen a more lovely princess.

The cat and his master had an even more delicious dinner that night, of fried fish, roast chicken and truffles, and the cat reported the King's conversation.

"But I can't possibly go to court," said the young man. "I haven't the right clothes. I'm not fit to meet a king or a princess. This is absurd. Where will it end?"

The next morning, after delivering his latest gift, a flock of pure white doves, the cat overheard the courtiers saying that the King and the Princess would ride in the royal carriage that afternoon.

They were to go along the river path, after the King visited his tailor to pick up his new suit.

The cat pranced back to the cave. "A bathe in the river for you this afternoon," he told his master. "I'll show you the exact spot. Leave everything to me."

"Really?" said the young man.

But he stepped into
the water happily, if a little
bewildered, while the cat secretly
hid his clothes.

As the royal carriage
approached, the cat screamed,
"HELP! HELP! The Marquis of
Carabas is DROWNING!"

"Oh, no!" called the King,
through his carriage window.

"Not the MARQUIS!" He halted the carriage, and sent two courtiers racing to the rescue.

"My poor master!" mourned the cat. "Some wicked robbers stole all his belongings while he was bathing, though I tried to stop them. He has no clothes!"

"Luckily," replied the King, "I have a new suit right here."

And as the young man approached the carriage, dripping wet and wrapped in the courtiers' cloaks, the King waved to him.

"Do borrow my spare clothes, Marquis, and join us for our afternoon outing."

"Thank you, Your Majesty," said the young man, and put on the King's magnificent outfit

He stepped into the warm carriage, and sank into soft velvet cushions, opposite the Princess. She was so friendly and charming that he fell instantly in love.

Meanwhile the cat ran ahead. He passed a large field full of workmen harvesting the corn and shouted: "Who owns this field?"

"The ogre," they replied.

"When the King comes by,
tell him this field belongs to the
Marquis of Carabas, or I'll have
you chopped into mincemeat."
The poor workmen were so
terrified at the sight of a talking
cat in boots that they
believed him. And
when the King called
from his carriage,

"Whose fine harvest is this?" they replied, "The Marquis of Carabas, Sire."

"Ah," said the King. By this time, the cat had raced down the road where endless green pastures dotted with sheep stretched to the far horizon.

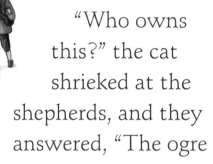

"Who owns this?" the cat shrieked at the shepherds, and they answered, "The ogre from the castle down the road."

"Tell the King, when he comes by, that it belongs to the Marquis of Carabas, or you'll be chopped into mincemeat, and eaten."

These shepherds were as terrified as the workmen, and promised to obey. So when the King asked them, "To whom do these pastures and sheep belong?" one answered nervously, "The Marquis of Carabas, Sire."

"Ah..." said the King, with a smile.

Now the cat whizzed like the wind to the ogre's castle. The cat knew that ogres could perform magic tricks, and that they ate children – but not, as far as he understood, cats. He rang the bell, and the ogre opened the door.

"WELL?" bellowed the ogre.

"How do you do? I am Puss in Boots," announced the cat.

Puss in Boots

"Tell me, is it true that you can change yourself into any animal you want, even a lion?"

The ogre nodded.

"That's the cleverest thing I've ever heard," sighed the cat in admiration. "It's hard to believe... Could you possibly show me?"

"Delighted."

The ogre grinned,
and Puss was
confronted by a
roaring lion.
Much alarmed, he
clambered up a wall, which was
difficult for him as his boots
slipped, until the ogre suddenly
resumed his normal form.

"Wonderful!" praised the cat.

"But I imagine, being so large yourself, you can only do large animals. I don't suppose you could turn yourself into something tiny, say, a mouse?"

"Oh, couldn't I? Just watch this!" boasted the ogre and instantly a little mouse scampered past the cat, who darted at it and killed it.

At that moment, the royal carriage trundled by. The cat flung open the castle door with a sweeping bow. "Welcome to the castle of the Marquis of Carabas!"

In went the King, the Princess and the miller's son. The castle was furnished with gold and silver, and on the table a sumptuous banquet was laid out.

The Princess looked even prettier among the castle's treasures, and the young man fell even more deeply in love.

"I am impressed, Marquis, with your estate and your castle," said the King. "Indeed, you are rich enough to marry my daughter."

"Sire," replied the young man, blushing furiously, "I cannot lie.

Much as I would love to marry
the Princess, I am not fit for her.
I'm not a Marquis. I'm a poor man."

"Explain yourself," ordered
the King and, when he'd heard
the whole story, he roared with
laughter. "You are
truthful and lucky,
my boy, and that's
good enough."

"But the castle must belong now to the ogre's relations," said the young man. "Not me."

"He doesn't have any left. He ate them all up," said the cat. "I won the castle by my own cleverness, and I give it to you."

"And I'll make you the Marquis of Carabas from this very minute," said the King.

Puss in Boots

"As for the cat, I'll make him Prime Minister, and he shall live in comfort for the rest of his life."

And so it was. The miller's son married the Princess and lived happily ever after, and everyone agreed that no kingdom was better governed than the one ruled by the brilliant brains of Puss in Boots.

LITTLE RED
RIDING HOOD

Once upon a time, a little girl lived with her mother in a cottage, covered in roses, at the edge of a deep, dark forest. On the other side of the forest was another cottage, and here lived the little girl's grandmother.

Grandmother loved her granddaughter so much that she wanted to give her a present.

"I'll make something myself, with my own hands," she thought. "What can I make that she doesn't already have?"

She sat by the fire, thinking hard, until at last she found the answer.

"I know! A red cloak with a hood, to keep her warm."

So she bought a roll of soft material, as red as a holly berry, with thread to match, and a length of scarlet ribbon.

When it was finished, the little girl put it on and said, "I'll never, ever take it off."

And, because she never did, everyone called her Little Red Riding Hood.

Not long after, Grandmother fell ill. Little Red Riding Hood's mother filled a basket with

 freshly baked cakes and elderberry cordial, and covered it with a clean, white cloth.

"I want you
to carry this to
Grandmother,"
she said.

"All by myself?"
asked Little Red Riding Hood.
"Through the forest?"

"Yes," said her mother.
"You'll be fine if you're careful."

"How will I be careful?"

"Just keep tight hold of the basket, and keep to the path. You know the way. There's nothing to worry about. Besides, today the forest is full of woodcutters, chopping down trees."

So Little Red Riding Hood carefully took the basket, closed the garden gate behind her and waved goodbye to her mother.

ff she went, following the forest path until she couldn't see her mother any more, or her cottage, or the gate. In a few moments she was surrounded by nothing but huge fir trees that made ghostly noises

Little Red Riding Hood

as their branches rubbed together.
The way in front grew dark as
night because the treetops hid
the sky. Ahead of her, it seemed
as if the entire forest was wearing
an inky black cloak with an inky
black hood. Only the occasional
patch of sunlight filtered through.

"I'm scared," whispered
Little Red Riding Hood.

She gripped the basket and listened to the trees moan. "But the forest is full of woodcutters," she reassured herself. "If I just keep to the path, soon I'll be at Grandmother's cottage where everything will be fine."

Little Red Riding Hood didn't know that hidden in the depths of the forest was a pack of wolves.

They slunk
between the
shadowy tree trunks, prowling
and stalking and hunting for
succulent, juicy, delicious…

Delicious what?

WAIT AND SEE.

Nor did Little Red Riding Hood
know that the wolves
were watching *her*.

Her red cloak was so bright, she glowed brighter than the berries.

She stopped for a moment to check her basket, and the biggest wolf turned around to grin at the other wolves with his sharp white teeth.

"MINE!" he hissed.

He stepped out of the shadows and stopped right in front of her.

Little Red Riding Hood

"Oh!" said Little Red Riding Hood in surprise. She had never seen a wolf before.

"Where are you going, you dear little girl?" asked the wolf in a soft voice. "And what are you carrying?"

"I'm taking cakes to my grandmother," replied Little Red Riding Hood. "We baked them yesterday, and they'll cheer her up.

She lives in the cottage with roses on the other side of the forest."

The wolf thought quickly, and as fast as his brain worked, his lips began to dribble. Then he licked them, once, twice, three times with his long red tongue.

"The young one would taste much better than the old one.

I must plot and plan, and then I can eat them both. I might even have the cakes too, for a treat."

He turned to Little Red Riding Hood and now his voice was so melting and sweet that it sounded like fudge and toffee and marshmallows warmed up and mixed together. "Goodness gracious me, little girl, you don't seem to be taking any notice of the wonderful flowers that are growing all around you." He cocked his head. "And I don't believe you're listening to the birds singing so charmingly in the trees."

Little Red Riding Hood glanced up to the topmost tree branches.

A single shaft of sunlight darted through the firs to the forest floor, making the flowers in its beam sparkle like jewels.

"Perhaps I should pick some flowers to take to Grandmother," said Little Red Riding Hood.

"What a good idea," the wolf burst out, nearly jumping up and down with impatience.

Little Red Riding
Hood ran to find the
prettiest flowers.
As soon as she
picked one, she spied
another a little farther off, and
soon she was deep in the heart
of the forest.

Meanwhile the wolf raced in great galloping strides to Grandmother's cottage and knocked at the door. Tap, tap, tap.

"Who's there?" Grandmother croaked, in her ill, quavery voice.

"It's your granddaughter, Little Red Riding Hood," called the wolf, trying to sound young and sweet. "I've brought cakes and cordial for you. Please open the door."

"Lift the latch," Grandmother called back. "I'm in bed. I'm not well enough to get up."

So the wolf lifted the latch, and burst through the door. In he ran, and gobbled Grandmother up. It didn't take long, because she was so old and thin. Then he put on her nightdress and her cap, and lay down in her bed, pulling up the covers as far as he could over his face. And he waited.

"Aha!" he chuckled. "Clever me. I'm the cleverest wolf in the whole wide world. I've laid my trap. One in my tum, and the best to come."

Soon there was a tap, tap, tap at the door.

"Who's there?" croaked the wolf, trying to sound old.

"It's your granddaughter,

Little Red Riding Hood. I've brought a basket of cakes and some cordial for you. Please open the door."

The wolf slid further down in the bed, almost purring now with excitement.

"Lift the latch, my dear, and come in. I'm in bed. I'm not well enough to get up."

Little Red Riding Hood opened the door, and went into her grandmother's cottage. She laid down her basket, and put her bunch of flowers in a vase, before taking a closer look at her grandmother.

"Grandmother looks a little strange today," she thought. "I wonder what it could be."

Little Red Riding Hood

She looked again. "Maybe it's because I've never seen her in her night things before. And she's ill, of course. Even so…"

And as Little Red Riding Hood stared, the wolf lay back on the old lady's soft white pillows thinking what a plump, juicy, sweet, delicious morsel was so very, very nearly in his grasp.

He sang a song to himself, in which the only words were Yum! Yum! Yum!

To hurry things up a little, he whispered, "Come right here, dear, and give me a hug."

Little Red Riding Hood snuggled up to the wolf and was even more bewildered.

"Grandmother has HAIR on her face! She smells! And everything about her is JUST NOT RIGHT."

"Oh Grandmother, what big ears you've got," she began.

"All the better to hear you with," hissed the wolf.

"Oh Grandmother, what huge eyes you've got."

"All the better to see you with," squealed the wolf.

"Oh Grandmother, what enormous hands you've got."

The wolf was hardly able to contain his excitement. "All the better to hold you with," he snarled. "But hasn't anyone ever told you not to make personal remarks?"

Little Red Riding Hood couldn't stop herself. "Oh Grandmother, what sharp teeth you've got."

At that, the wolf leaped out of bed, bellowing, "All the better to EAT YOU UP!"

He opened his huge mouth as wide as he could and grabbed Little Red Riding Hood in his strong, hairy paws.

Little Red Riding Hood

She let out a scream: "AAAAAHHHH!!!!!" and in one great, gulping mouthful, he swallowed her whole. Then he lay down again on the bed, but instead of feeling happy and full, as he'd expected, his stomach throbbed and heaved and he had a bad tummy-ache.

"OH! OW!" he groaned.

One of the woodcutters working in the forest had heard the scream. Now he heard nothing but deep, whimpering moans, one after the other.

"What a noise the old woman is making," he said to himself.

"I'd better see if there's anything the matter with her."

He ran to Grandmother's cottage, opened the door and found the wolf writhing on the bed, howling in pain and with a very full tummy.

"I can guess what you've done, you old villain," said he. "I'll have to rescue them."

Little Red Riding Hood

He slit open the wolf's body and there was Little Red Riding Hood. "Oh, I'm so glad to be out," she cried.

Then out came Grandmother, and she said, "At least it was warm, dear. There's always something to be grateful for, though it's not an experience I would wish to repeat."

Little Red Riding Hood ran outside and found some large stones which she put into the wolf's body, and then Grandmother sewed up the slit with some leftover scarlet thread that she'd bought to make Little Red Riding Hood's cloak.

After that, the wolf couldn't walk without rattling, which gave everyone warning that he was near. And the rest of the wolves saw what would happen if they ate people, so the forest became an almost safe place for anyone strolling through it.

Almost.

A few days later, another wolf stopped Little Red Riding Hood on her way to visit her grandmother. "Come with me. We can explore the forest together," he murmured.

But this time Little Red Riding Hood was wise. She took no notice of him at all.

Little Red Riding Hood

In the end, the wolf disappeared back into the darkness of the trees. Skip, skip, skip, went Little Red Riding Hood, all the way down the forest path to Grandmother, who was feeling much better, and skip, skip, skip back home again.

ABOUT THE STORIES

People have been telling and retelling the stories in this book for hundreds of years. The stories changed a little with each new telling, so nowadays there are many different versions of them.

Most fairytales are so old,
no one knows who the original
authors were. The oldest
version of Cinderella comes
from Ancient Egypt. But many
talented storytellers
have helped to make
fairytales popular
over the centuries.

They include the Brothers
Grimm in Germany, Hans
Christian Andersen in Denmark,
and Charles Perrault in France.

This book continues the
tradition by retelling five of
the most popular fairytales for
readers today.

Edited by Lesley Sims and Rosie Dickins
Designed by Nancy Leschnikoff and Vickie Robinson
Digital image manipulation: Nick Wakeford

First published in 2017 by Usborne Publishing Ltd.,
83-85 Saffron Hill, London, EC1N 8RT, England.
www.usborne.com.Copyright © 2017, 2015 Usborne Publishing Ltd.
The name Usborne and the devices ♀ ⊕ are Trade Marks of
Usborne Publishing Ltd.